Adventures of
Abby and The seahorse

make cheese

Beth Phillips

To order additional copies of this book, contact:
Xlibris
844-714-8691
www.Xlibris.com
Orders@Xlibris.com

ISBN: Softcover   978-1-6698-0608-0
        EBook   978-1-6698-0609-7

Print information available on the last page

Rev. date: 01/07/2021

Grateful acknowledgements to:

CEM Corporation and God.

This book belongs to:

There are many standards
in different arenas of life.
Dog shows for example.
This is the standardization
step in cheese making.

Many things begin with

similar words to pastures.

Famous artists, etc.

This is the pasteurization step.

There are many venues

that require starters.

Including the noble game of golf.

Starter Culture

Abby and the seahorse get Coagulated.

Abby and the seahorse get Cooked.

Abby and the seahorse are

examined for a protein analysis.

Just like teeth are extracted, so is whey.

Abby and the seahorse get salted.

Abby and the seahorse get ripened.

Ready for Abby and the seahorse bread.

Scrambled Packaging.

Abby and the seahorse are

excited to be Distributed.

The tires turn into donuts and Abby and the seahorse offer them to the store manager.

References:

1. CEM Corporation, ISO certification since 1994, sponsor: not listed, date viewed: Dec 26, 2021.

Printed in the United States
by Baker & Taylor Publisher Services